I Love KINDERGARTEN!
NUMBERS

To the teachers who make math fun—DJS

For Aser and Mai—LM

GROSSET & DUNLAP
An imprint of Penguin Random House LLC
1745 Broadway, New York, New York 10019

First published in the United States of America by Grosset & Dunlap,
an imprint of Penguin Random House LLC, 2025

Text copyright © 2025 by D. J. Steinberg
Illustrations copyright © 2025 by Leire Martín

Penguin Random House values and supports copyright. Copyright fuels creativity, encourages diverse voices, promotes free speech, and creates a vibrant culture. Thank you for buying an authorized edition of this book and for complying with copyright laws by not reproducing, scanning, or distributing any part of it in any form without permission. You are supporting writers and allowing Penguin Random House to continue to publish books for every reader. Please note that no part of this book may be used or reproduced in any manner for the purpose of training artificial intelligence technologies or systems.

GROSSET & DUNLAP is a registered trademark of Penguin Random House LLC.

Visit us online at penguinrandomhouse.com.

Library of Congress Cataloging-in-Publication Data is available.

Manufactured in China

ISBN 9780593754436   10 9 8 7 6 5 4 3 2 1 HH

Design by Skyler Kratofil

NUMBERS

BY D. J. STEINBERG
ILLUSTRATED BY LEIRE MARTÍN

GROSSET & DUNLAP

NUMBERS EVERYWHERE

The world is filled with numbers,
everywhere you look . . .
on the classroom walls, the tables,
in the corners of this book.
Anywhere you go,
you are guaranteed to need 'em.
That's why in kindergarten math,
we're learning how to read 'em!

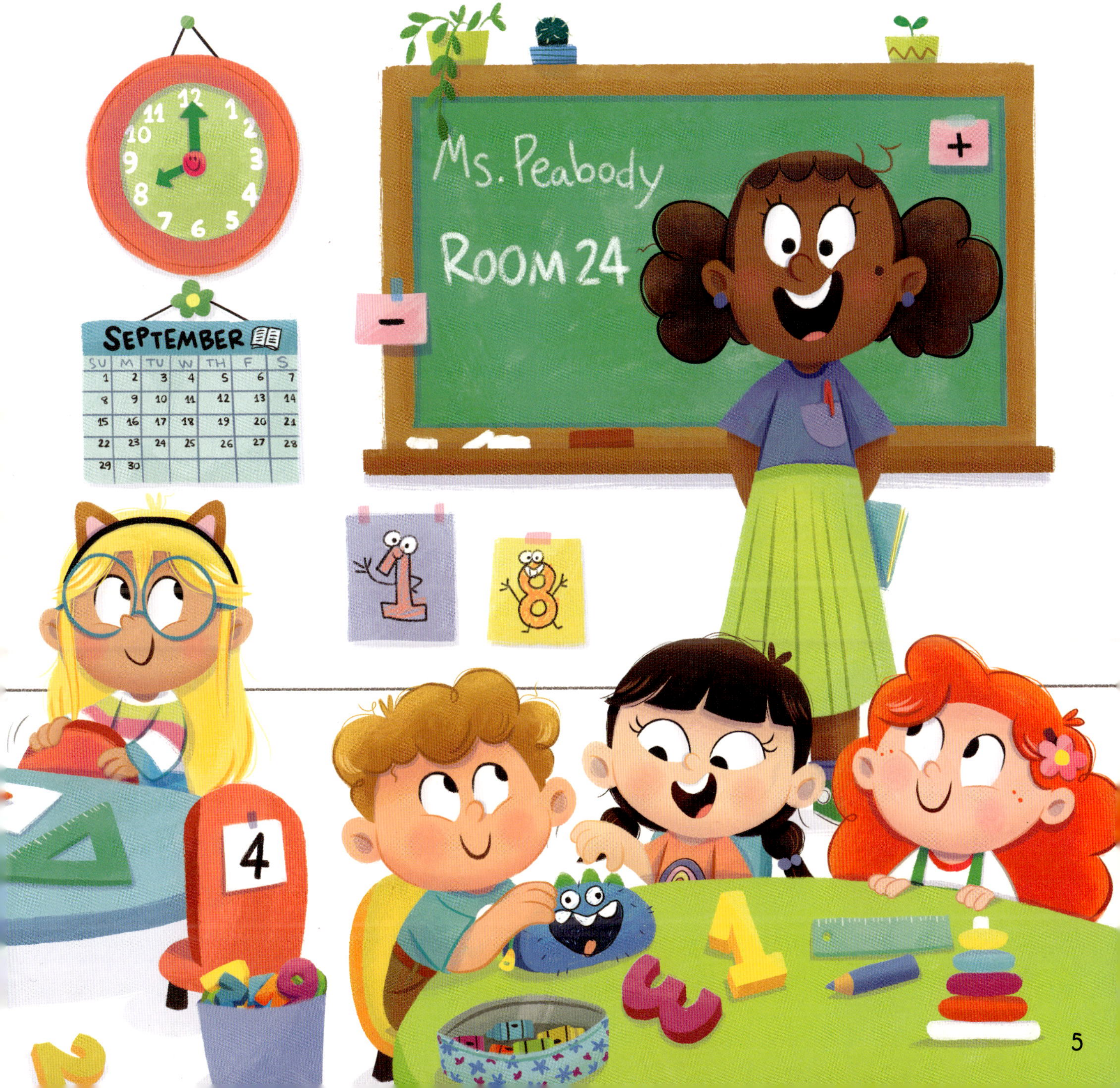
Ms. Peabody
ROOM 24
SEPTEMBER
SU M TU W TH F S
1 2 3 4 5 6 7
8 9 10 11 12 13 14
15 16 17 18 19 20 21
22 23 24 25 26 27 28
29 30
4

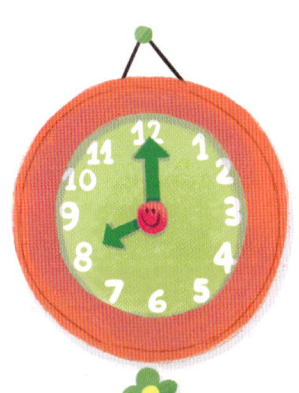

NUMBER HUNT

In the morning on the school bus,
we play a game that's fun.
We hunt for numbers on the streets,
starting out with *one*.

We find a *two*, then *three*, then *four* . . .
and right on up to *ten*.
When we find them all, *we win*—
and start from *one* again!

CAN'T STOP COUNTING!

Help! I can't stop counting!
I count everything I see—
flowers, trees, and friends . . .
Will you count them all with me?

STAY, FISH, STAY!

How many fish are in the tank?
I've tried to count them all day,
but whenever I start counting,
those fish keep swimming away!

THREE GUESSES . . .

I live on Third Street, number 33,
on the third floor with my family—
three brothers, three sisters, three kittens, and me.
Three guesses what my favorite number might be?!

FINGERS AND TOES

I use my fingers to count to ten
and my toes to count to twenty, but then
if I have to count any higher than those,
I might need to borrow *your* fingers and toes!

DINOSAUR PARADE

Here come the dinosaurs, one and all.
We line them up from big to small.
Across the playtime rug they go,
dinos marching in a row.

But *wait*, hold on. There's something wrong . . .
Where does that *T. rex* belong?

SORTING IT OUT

After lunch, we sort our trash.
We have to pick the right bin.
Paper, plastic, or leftover food . . .
Which bin does *this* go in?

MY OTHER BOOT

Where did my other boot go?
It must be here somewhere.
I can't go out with only one boot!
Will you help me find its pair?

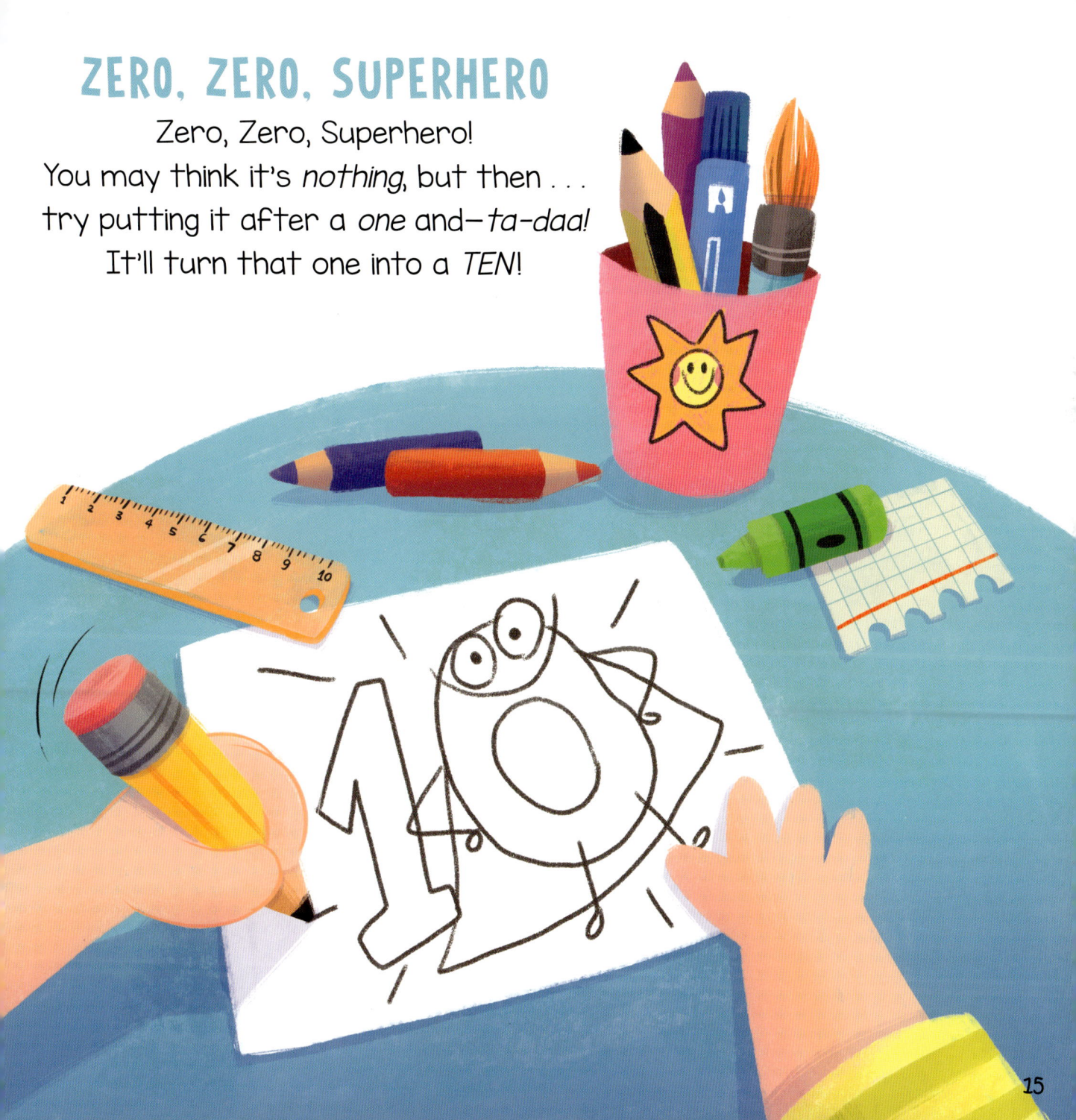

ZERO, ZERO, SUPERHERO

Zero, Zero, Superhero!
You may think it's *nothing*, but then . . .
try putting it after a *one* and—*ta-daa!*
It'll turn that one into a *TEN*!

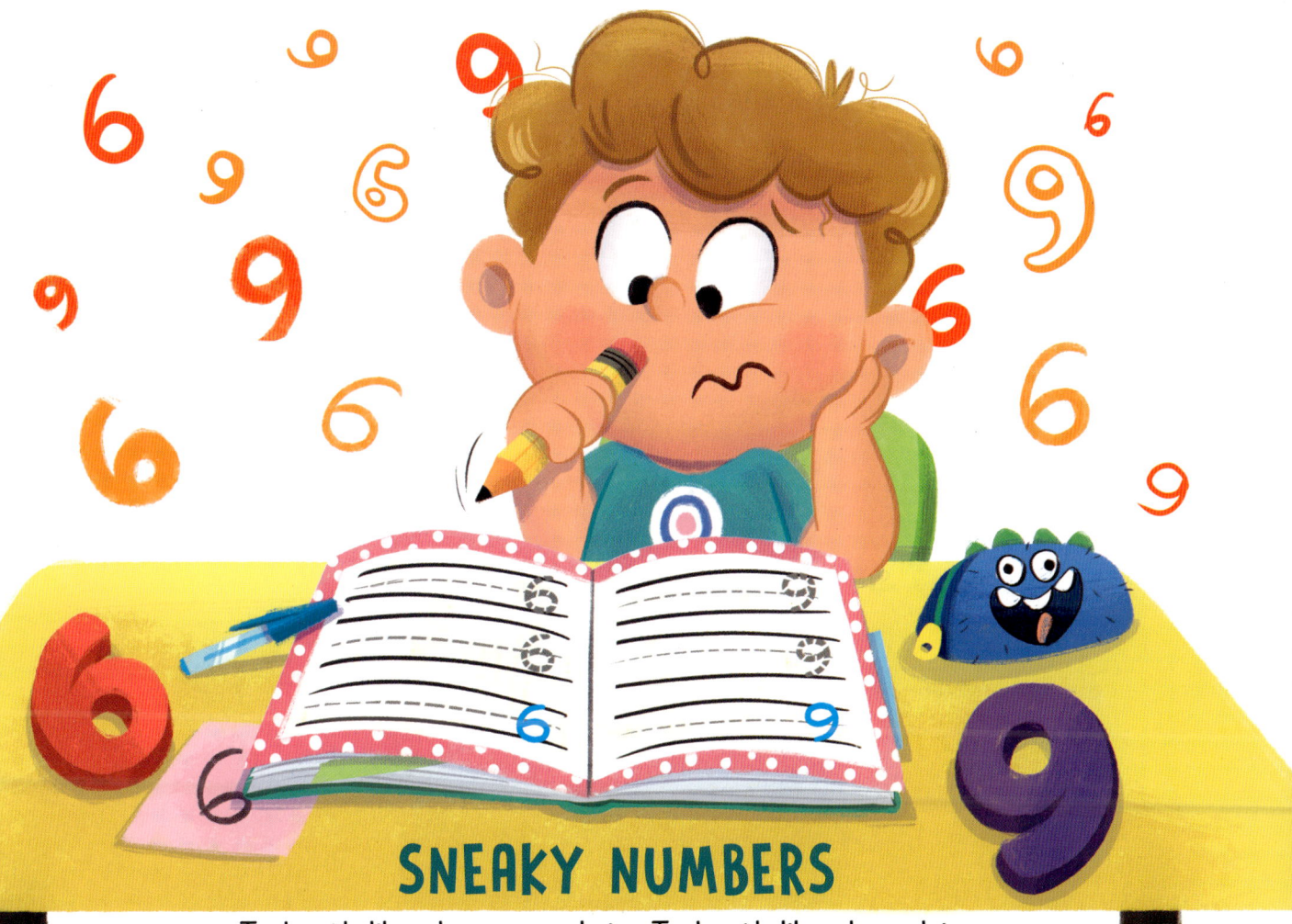

SNEAKY NUMBERS

I don't like to complain, I don't like to whine,
but I'm having some trouble with 6 and 9.
Those sneaky numbers are full of tricks,
'cause upside-down, that 9 makes a 6!
And an upside-down 6 makes a 9... *oh, great!*
Why can't those numbers be more like an 8?

COOKIE MATH

My lunch box has only *one* cookie,
so I trade my chips with Drew.
He gives me his cookie . . . What does that make?
$1 + 1 = 2$

My tummy still needs some more cookies,
so I trade my raisins with Lee.
I eat up her cookie . . . What does that make?
$2 + 1 = 3$

Three is *still* not enough cookies,
so I trade apple slices with Jake.
He gives me a cookie . . . Now, what does that make?

. . . A big old TUMMY ACHE!

SHAPE MAGIC

Ladies and gentlemen, for my next trick,
I'll take this perfect *SQUARE*.
I fold it in half and—*abracadabra!*
Now a *TRIANGLE* is there!

TA-DAAA

RAINY DAY RECESS

Sometimes when it's raining,
we go bowling in the hall.
Our teacher sets TEN pins up.
We take turns rolling the ball.
Jackie's first. "Watch this!" she says.
The rest of the class keeps score.

CIRCLE POEM

Cinnamon waffles and steamy pancakes, chocolate-chip cookies my daddy bakes, pita bread, pennies and pickle jar tops, smiley-face buttons and red lollipops, a pizza pie dotted with round pepperonis, a pink hula-hoop, a slice of baloney, bicycle tires that twirl and spin, around and around like this poem that I'm in!

SNACK O'CLOCK

When the big hand's on the twelve
and the little hand's on the ten,
that means it's ten o'clock
and guess what happens then?!

WHAT BEAD COMES NEXT?

Check out this bracelet I'm making
with beads from my teacher's jar.
I'm stringing them up in a *pattern*—
a circle, a square, then a star.
A pattern is when you repeat a design,
so I pick out more beads carefully—
a circle, a square, then a star again . . .
Do you see what the next bead should be?

26

ONE HUNDREDTH DAY OF SCHOOL

I brought one hundred pennies
in ten neat rows of ten.
They're taped up on a poster
and numbered with a pen.
You should have seen kids' faces.
"You're *rich*!" I heard them holler,
because one hundred pennies are the same
as *one whole dollar*!

IT MAKES NO *CENTS*!

Whenever I try counting change,
I get into a pickle—
if a dime is worth ten cents,
why's it smaller than the nickel?
A nickel's worth just *five* cents,
which makes *no* sense—*excuse me?*
Who made the dime so tiny?
Are they trying to confuse me?!

HURRAY—IT'S MAY!

Today is the start of the very best month.
It's the very first day of May.
Now I just have to count *one-two-three-four* more days
to the best day of all—*my BIRTHDAY!*

PICKUP TIME

5 of us are waiting.
One dad is at the door.
We wave goodbye to Tina
and now there are **4**.

4 of us are waiting.
Look—what do we see?
The bus is here! *Bye-bye, Raj* . . .
And now there are **3**.

3 of us are waiting.
We hear a loud *"Yoo-hoo!"*
Stephaney grabs her backpack
and now there are **2**.

2 of us are waiting—
my friend's wait is all done.
Brady's carpool has arrived
and now there's only **1**.

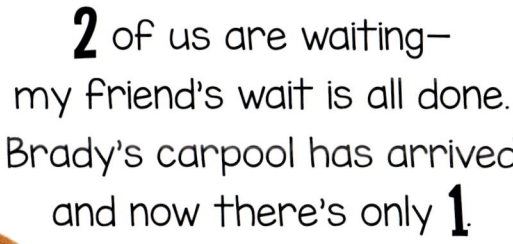

1 of us is waiting—*me!*
Hey—here comes someone . . .
My mama gives me a big hug
and now there are *none!*